W9-DEI-227

WITHDRAWN

SEP 19 2024

NAFC PUBLIC LIBRARY

YP SU
Sudduth, Brent H., 1964-
Superman : doom in a box / w
M   343270        12/10/08

# Superman™
## Doom in a Box

Copyright © DC Comics 2008. First Edition,
Printed in The United States of America. All rights reserved.
ISBN: 978-0-696-23956-4

Superman and all related names, characters, and elements
are trademarks of DC Comics © 2008.
All rights reserved.
Superman created by Jerry Siegel and Joe Shuster.

We welcome your comments and suggestions.
Write to us at: Meredith Books, Children's Books,
1716 Locust Street, Des Moines, IA 50309-3023

Visit us at: meredithbooks.com

Written by Brent Sudduth
Illustrated by Dan Panosian

It was another busy day at the *Daily Planet* in Metropolis, where Clark Kent just finished typing his latest news story. *Whew, just before deadline*, Clark thought.

"Hey, Clark, you seem a bit too happy for my taste," Lois pointed out. "What's the story?"

"Oh, no story, Lois, just my latest column," Clark explained. "What's the Chief have you working on?"

Before Lois could answer, Jimmy Olsen arrived and dropped a gift-wrapped box onto Clark's desk.

"Hey, Mr. Kent! You have a present," said Jimmy, "straight from the mailroom."

*A present?* Clark wondered. He leaned forward and unwrapped the box.

"From a secret admirer, Clark?" Lois quipped.

"Kent! Kent!" shouted Perry White, Editor-in-Chief of the *Daily Planet*. "Why am I not editing your column? It's late!"

"This is so cool," Jimmy said as he finished opening Clark's gift. "Look, Mr. Kent! It's an action figure of—of Doomsday. It looks so *real*." Jimmy dangled the toy in the air as its arms and legs began to move.

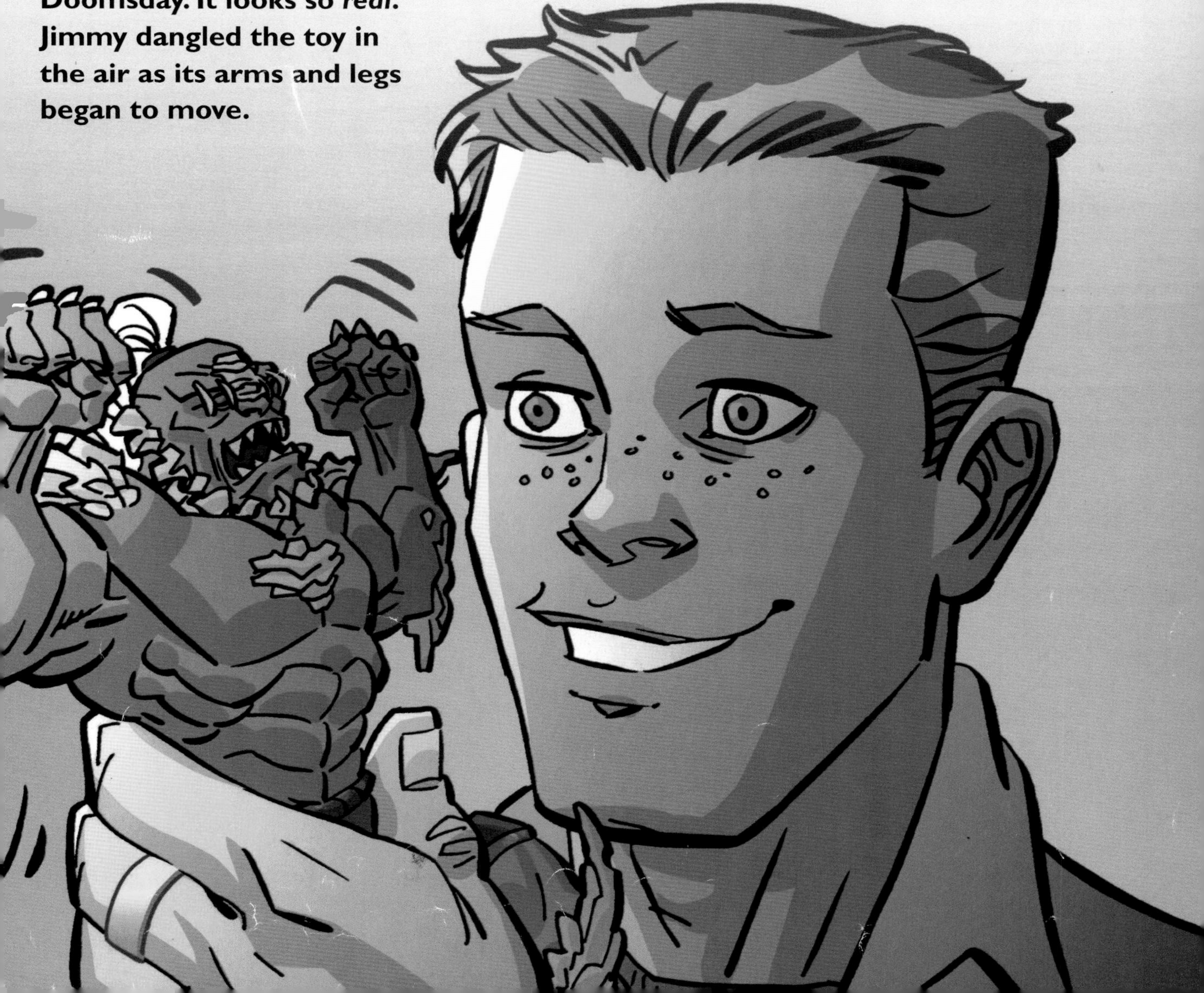

"Olsen! Where are those pictures? Put that down and get me pictures!" grumbled Perry.

"Ok, ok! Sorry, Chief! Really cool toy, Mr. Kent," Jimmy said as he reached to give it back. "Oops!" Jimmy said as the toy slipped out of his fingers and into a glass of water on Clark's desk.

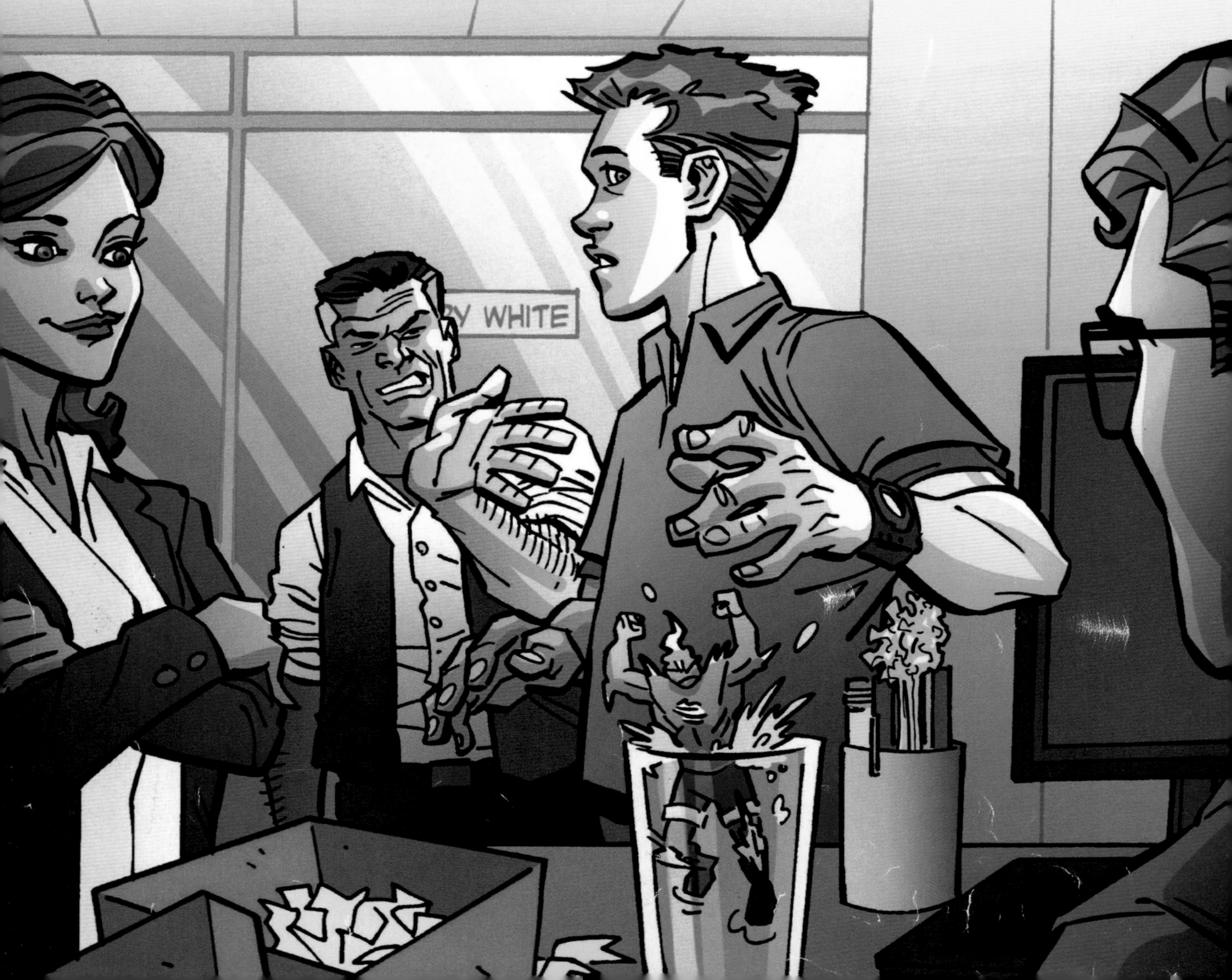
WHITE

"Sorry about that, Mr. Kent," he said.

"Now *there's* a story, Smallville," Lois chimed in.

"*I Trapped Doomsday in a Glass of Water,* by Clark Kent."

"Kent, in my office—now!" ordered Perry.

"Sure thing, Chief," Clark answered.

"Oh wait, I forgot my camera case," said Jimmy as he turned back toward Clark's desk. "Hey, Mr. Kent! Why's your desk shaking?" he asked. Suddenly the toy Doomsday began to grow—and grow—and grow!

"**RRRR—RRRAAH!**" roared the suddenly life-size toy.

"**D-Doomsday!**" Jimmy exclaimed. Nervously, he started taking pictures of the toy as it transformed into the powerful villain.

"**Jimmy! Watch out!**" yelled Lois, as Doomsday loomed over the young photographer.

"Whoooaaa!" Jimmy yelped as a strong wind swept under his feet. With everyone distracted, Clark secretly used his superbreath and blew Jimmy right out of the clutches of the raging Doomsday.

"Everyone out of the building!" shouted Clark.

"Go! Go! Go!" Clark yelled as he helped Jimmy, Lois, and Perry into an elevator.

"But Clark, what about you?" asked Lois. It was too late. The doors shut, and Clark turned around and ran down the hallway.

*I have to move fast, or Doomsday's going to be*—but Clark never finished the thought. **"GGRrRAAaRRKK!"** Doomsday crashed through the door.

Superman flew high over the Metropolis streets to escape Doomsday's rampage. Trying to grab Superman, Doomsday leapt at him but fell short.

*Oh no! There are people below!* realized Superman. He flew at superspeed and scooped up bystanders just as Doomsday crashed to the street.

Superman blasted Doomsday with his heat vision. The heat only made the monster angrier.

"Great Caesar's Ghost!" exclaimed Perry. "Will nothing slow him down?"

Barely able to stop Doomsday, Superman struggled to keep him under control. Just then a huge stream of water hit the raging creature.

"We'll help you, Superman!" said the group of firefighters hosing down Doomsday.

In disbelief Superman watched as Doomsday started growing again! Bigger and **bigger** and **bigger** until he was as tall as a skyscraper.

*What is going on here?* puzzled Superman. *Water makes him grow?* The now-gigantic Doomsday batted Superman right out of the sky and through a toy store's window.

*I've got to find a way to lead him out of the city before he destroys Metropolis,* thought a dazed Superman. As he crawled out of the rubble, Superman spied something startling.

"Oh no! Look at all of these Doomsday toys. Could they *all* be like this? This would mean *thousands* of Doomsdays," Superman said.

*Wait a second!* Superman realized. *This isn't the real Doomsday—it's a toy! These are all toys. And that means I know who is behind this: Toyman.* Using his superspeed, the Last Son of Krypton gathered all the dangerous toys in his cape and took to the sky.

Using his superhearing, Superman listened for a signal.
Toyman must be controlling this Doomsday by a radio
frequency, Superman reasoned. *I just have to listen well
enough and I can trace it back to him.*

"Come on, big guy! Follow me this way," Superman called to the enormous toy.

"RRR-RRAAARRR!!" the Doomsday toy raged. Superman dodged every move it made as the massive toy crashed through Metropolis trying to catch him.

The Man of Steel lured the giant out of the city to a nearby abandoned factory. *There you are,* thought Superman as his X-ray vision revealed Toyman inside. *Time to return your gift.*

Superman crashed through the wall, catching Toyman at the controls of the gigantic monster.

"Hi, Toyman," Superman said. "I brought an old friend for you to play with."

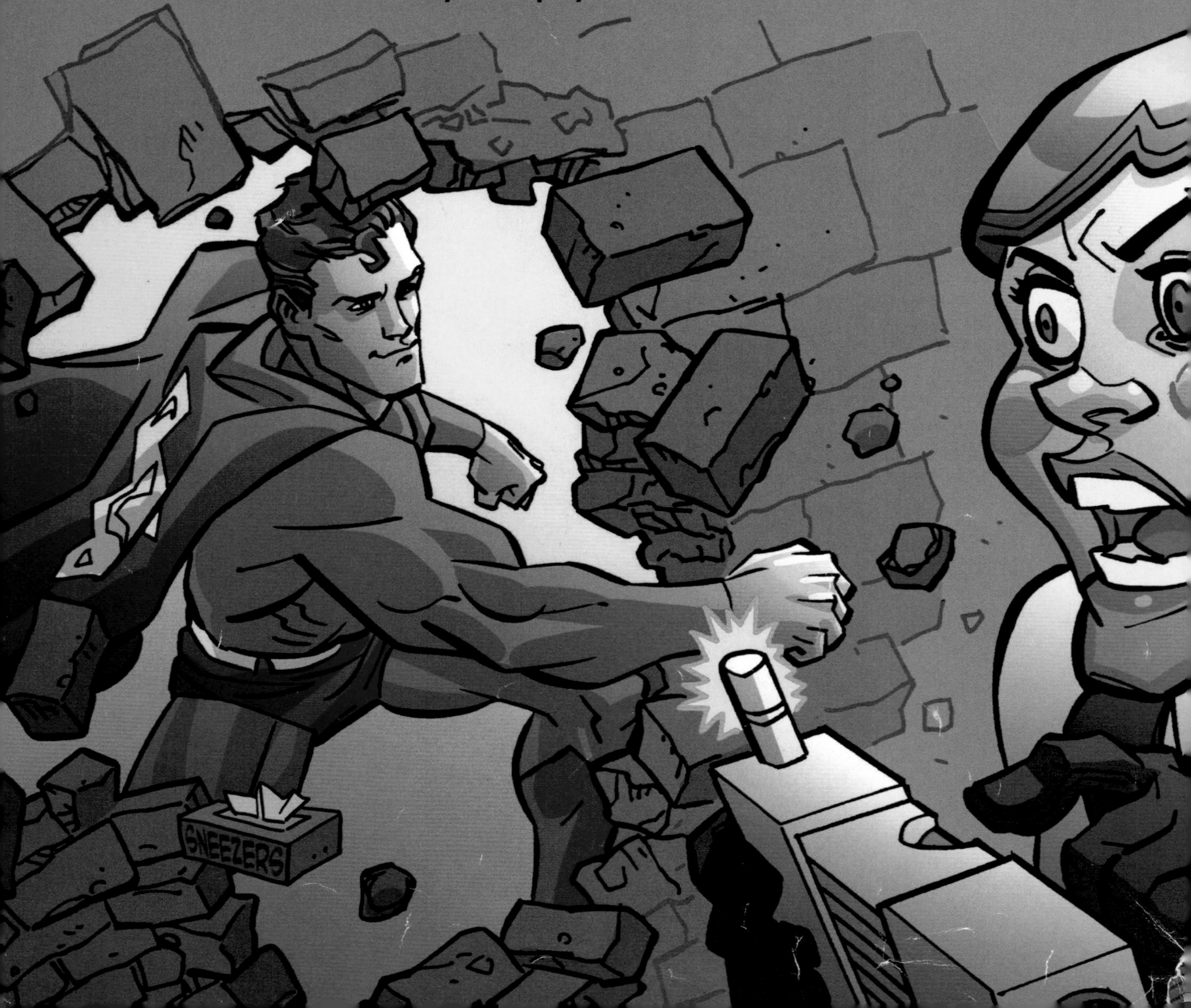
SNEEZERS

The colossal Doomsday toy crashed through the factory ceiling.

"And that's enough of that," said Superman as he used his heat vision to melt the controller in Toyman's hands. "Your other toys are gone, too. There will be no more doom in a box from you."

# ATTENTION, METROPOLIS CITIZENS!

Toyman has hidden the items below throughout Metropolis. We here at the *Daily Planet* are asking you to help Superman find them. Be careful—these items are dangerous, and one of them is hidden on each page.

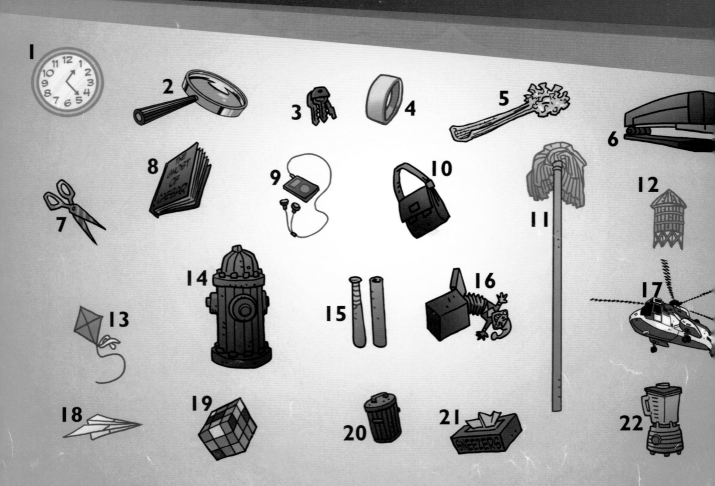